When Giants Come to Play

written by **Andrea Beaty**
illustrated by **Kevin Hawkes**

Abrams Books for Young Readers
New York

To the giants in my life—Katie, Andrew, Michael—
and most especially—my mom and dad
—A.B.

To Josh and Brooke, true giants
—K.H.

Artist's Note:

The illustrations in this book were created using charcoal pencils
and acrylic paint on hundred-pound Bristol paper.

Author's Acknowledgments:

With many thanks to Barry Goldblatt and Susan Van Metre—giants both

This book was made possible, in part, by a Barbara Karlin Grant
from the Society of Children's Book Writers and Illustrators.

Designer: Vivian Cheng
Production Manager: Alexis Mentor

Library of Congress Cataloging-in-Publication Data has been applied for.
ISBN 13: 978-0-8109-5759-6
ISBN 10: 0-8109-5759-0

Printed and bound in China
10 9 8 7 6 5 4 3 2 1

HNA
harry n. abrams, inc.
a subsidiary of La Martinière Groupe
115 West 18th Street
New York, NY 10011
www.hnabooks.com

Sometimes, on a summer morning,
when the sun shines just so
and the wind blows like this and like that
on its way to somewhere else,
giants come to play.
They come to play with Anna
who waits for them just beyond the end of Lillian Lane.

When giants come to play, they hide and seek.
Anna knows lots of good places to hide.

When giants come to play, they shoot marbles in the park,
though they never play for keeps.

On mild days, they gather flowers in the garden.

On wild days, they play catch by the gnarled oak tree.

When giants come to play, they jump rope and sing.
Even the neighbors like to watch.

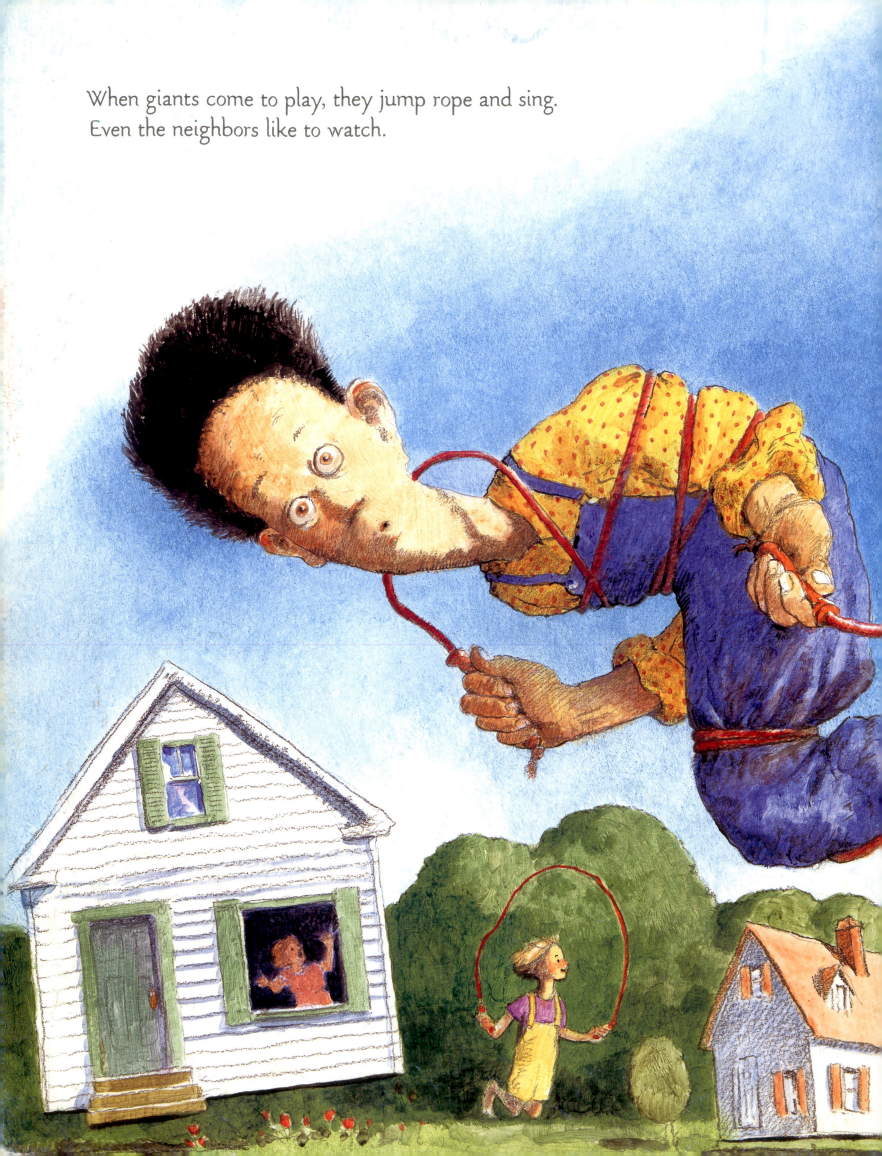

Then, as the midday sun spreads itself like a blanket over the grass,
Anna and the giants share mint tea and cakes that drip chocolate frosting.
Giants never make a mess.

When giants come to play, they pick peaches on the hillside and send seeds soaring through the summer sky.

When giants come to play, they race with Anna through the meadow.
It makes the giants happy when she lets them win.

Sometimes, they play dolls with Anna's sister.

Other times, they race cars with Anna's brother.

When giants come to play, they dangle their toes in the cool shady pond
and whisper secrets until their shadows grow long and sleepy.

At last the crickets bring out their fiddles
and milk-white moths dance for the stars
and Anna and the giants say, "Good night."

Then, sometimes, on a summer night,
when the moon shines just so
and the wind blows like that and like this
on its way home from somewhere else,
Anna drifts to sleep smiling.
She smiles *not* because giants come to play,
but because, she hopes . . .

. . . they've come to stay.

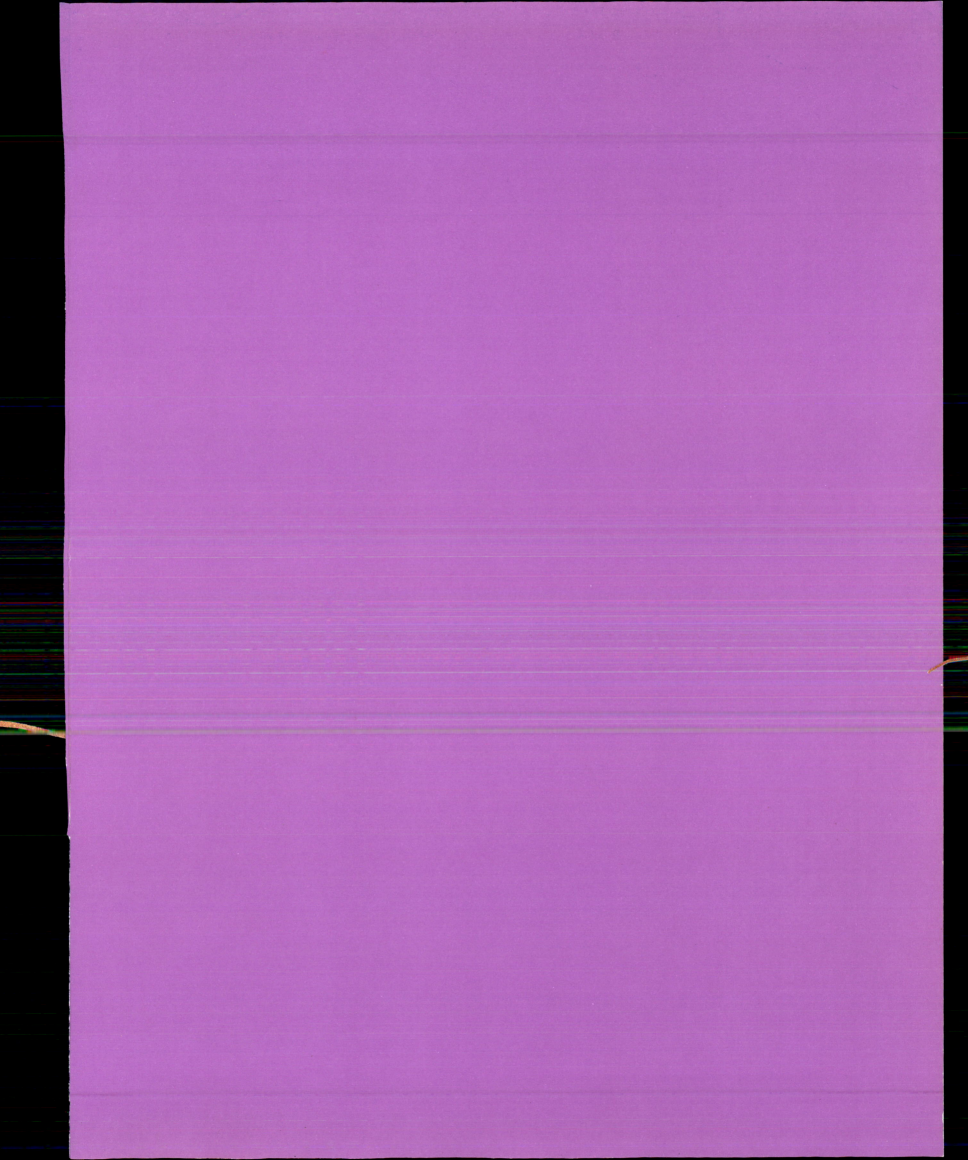